Favorite Fairy
The Pied Piper

Retold by Rochelle Larkin　　**Illustrated by Alan Leiner**

CREATIVE CHILD PRESS
is a registered trademark of Playmore Inc.,
Publishers and Waldman Publishing Corp., New York, N.Y.

Once upon a time there was a pretty little town called
Hamelin. The people were prosperous and the streets and houses
were clean and sturdy. But Hamelin had a horrible problem.

Rats! They ran in the streets. They filled the houses, spoiled the food, frightened the children, and generally made life miserable for everyone.

Now, the people of Hamelin hated to give away money, but finally they had to offer a reward to anyone who could rid them of the rats.

Many came, and many tried. But nothing anyone did was any help at all. The rats just got bigger and bolder.

The mayor offered even more money, but no one came to help for a long time.

Then one day a most unusual figure appeared. His clothes were many different colors and patterns, and he carried nothing but one long thin box.

He went to the mayor at once.

"For the three bags of gold you offer, I'll rid you of the rats," he said.

"Done!" said the mayor. The people were thrilled. They crowded at their windows and balconies and on the rooftops to watch as the stranger started playing his pipes.

The piper walked towards the outskirts of the town, piping away as he went. From the streets and the gutters and the houses, dozens and hundreds and thousands of rats came streaming out after him.

Away into the countryside the piper piped and the rats followed right behind. Not a single one stayed in Hamelin.

The piper kept going until he came to the river that flowed past the town. He stepped just a bit into the water and piped a little louder.

Soon all the rats went rushing into the stream and were drowned.

The pied piper went back to Hamelin. The town was clean. The people were happy. The mayor was waiting. He held a bag of gold in his hand.

"For just piping a little tune," the mayor said, "and taking a little walk, three bags of gold is too much. You can have one."

The pied piper was furious. "You promised three," he said. "I promised to rid you of all the rats, and I did. Now you must do as you promised."

"Not at all," said the mayor. "All the rats are gone, and you can take this one bag of gold and be gone too."

"I'll be gone," said the piper, "but so will all your children!"

With that, he began to play a different tune. And all at once, from the houses and the school rooms, from the playgrounds and the toy shops, the children of Hamelin appeared.

Once again the pied piper walked to the edge of the town, and all of the children followed. The older ones skipped and ran alongside. The babies crawled if they could, or were carried by their sisters and brothers, but none stayed behind.

Their parents ran after them, but it was no use. Mothers and fathers cried out to their children, but it was as if they couldn't hear them. On they went, towards the river of Hamelin.

All the people turned to the mayor.
"This is your fault!" they shouted. "Give him his money. Give us back our children!"

Still the mayor hesitated. "Maybe if I offer him two bags," he said slowly.

But the pied piper wouldn't hear of it.
"Three bags," he said, "a bargain is a bargain. Or else I keep the children and bring back the rats!"

"Oh, no!" they all cried out at once, even the mayor's wife.

"Three bags," said the piper, and he put his pipe to his mouth, ready to play.

"Two and a half bags?" asked the mayor meekly.

"Three bags!" shouted the mayor's wife and all the townspeople with her.

The piper blew a note. The music drifted on the air. The children started to walk.

"Three bags!" shouted the mayor, and the piper stopped playing and smiled.

The piper got his money and the rats were gone, the children came back, and they all lived to tell their own children, and their children's children ever after, about the day they followed the pied piper from Hamelin town.